Double Dip

Candy Fairies

Double Dip

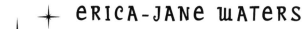

HELEN PERELMAN

ILLUSTRATED BY
ERICA-JANE WATERS

ALADDIN
NEW YORK   LONDON   TORONTO   SYDNEY   NEW DELHI

ALADDIN

An imprint of Simon & Schuster Children's Publishing Division

1230 Avenue of the Americas, New York, NY 10020

First Aladdin hardcover edition October 2012

Text copyright © 2012 by Helen Perelman

Illustrations copyright © 2012 by Erica-Jane Waters

For information about special discounts for bulk purchases, please contact Simon & Schuster Special Sales at 1-866-506-1949 or business@simonandschuster.com.

The Simon & Schuster Speakers Bureau can bring authors to your live event.

For more information or to book an event, contact the Simon & Schuster Speakers Bureau at 1-866-248-3049 or visit our website at www.simonspeakers.com.

Designed by Karina Granda

The text of this book was set in Berthold Baskerville Book.

Manufactured in the United States of America 0812 FFG

2 4 6 8 10 9 7 5 3 1

Library of Congress Control Number 2012941059

ISBN 978-1-4424-5972-4 (hc)

ISBN 978-1-4424-2219-3 (pbk)

ISBN 978-1-4424-2220-9 (eBook)

For Rachel, who discovered the healing power
of mint ice cream sandwiches!

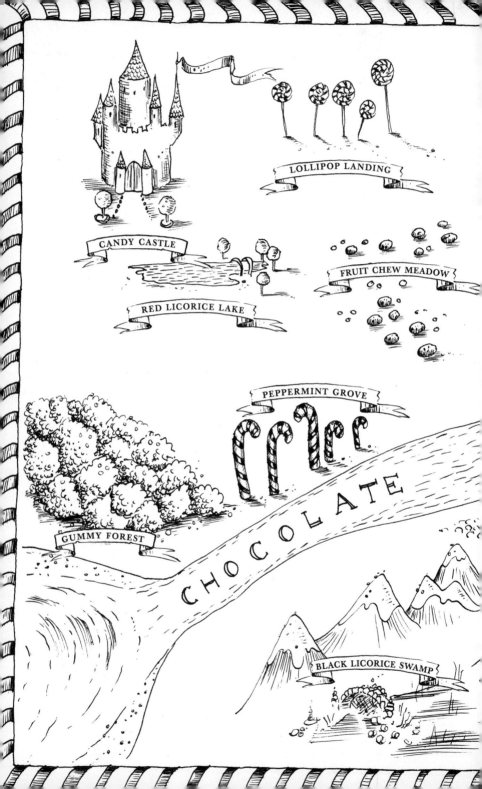

Contents

CHAPTER
1

Master of Mint

The sweet smell of peppermint made Dash's silver wings flutter. The small Mint Fairy was tending to her candies in Peppermint Grove. The weather was turning a little cooler, and there were many mint candies sprouting on the vines. This was perfect mint-chip weather! Dash picked a tiny mint pod from a stem in front of her. Carefully, she opened up the green pod, plucked the tiny mint chips out, and popped them into her mouth. "Mmm," she said. "Just right!"

"How are the new chips?" asked Minny. The young Mint Fairy flew over to Dash. "I've been waiting for those to ripen. How do they taste?"

"Perfect," Dash reported happily. She handed a pod to Minny. "Let me know what you think."

Minny put a handful of chips in her mouth and quickly agreed. "Yum, these are good," she said. "Dash, you are the master of mint!"

Dash blushed. She was excited about the mini mint chips. She thought they'd be perfect toppings for chocolates or even for ice cream. Just thinking about the yummy treats made her stomach rumble.

"Maybe we should take a break for lunch," Dash suggested. She rubbed her belly. "I'm starving."

Minny laughed. "Dash, you are always hungry!"

Dash couldn't argue. "I might be small, but I do have a huge appetite!" she said, laughing.

There wasn't a candy in Sugar Valley that Dash didn't love . . . although some she liked more than others!

The two Mint Fairies settled down under the shade of a few large peppermint leaves. Dash was thankful for the rest—and the delicious fruit nectar that she had brought for lunch.

"Oh, look, Dash!" Minny exclaimed. "There's a sugar fly note for you." She pointed to the fly circling over Dash's head.

Sugar flies brought messages to fairies throughout Sugar Valley. The flies could spread information—or gossip— to fairies far and wide. Dash quickly opened the note and then flew straight up in the air.

"Holy peppermint!" she cried. She zoomed around and then did a somersault.

"What did that note say?" Minny asked. She leaped up in excitement. "Must be extra-sweet news."

Dash flew back down to the ground. "I just got the best invitation," she told her friend. "You will not believe this. *I* can't believe this!" She shot up in the air again.

"What?" Minny begged. "Come down and tell me!"

"This is *so mint!*" Dash gushed. "Wait till all my friends hear about this!" She scribbled off a note and handed it back to the sugar fly. "Please take this back to Meringue Island as fast as possible," Dash instructed. "My answer is YES!"

Minny's eyes grew wide. "Meringue Island?" she said. "Why, that's all the way in the Vanilla Sea!"

"Yes," Dash said. "And right near Mt. Ice Cream."

Clapping her hands, Minny cheered. "I know—were you invited to race in Double Dip?" she shouted.

"Sure as sugar!" Dash said, flipping in the air again.

"Dash, that is minty cool!" Minny exclaimed. "I've only read about that race. And now you are going to be in it!"

"I can't believe it," Dash repeated, landing back down on the ground.

Minny sighed. "I've never been all the way to Meringue Island," she said wistfully. "I've heard that the Cone Harbor Festival weekend is supersweet. They have all these amazing flavors of ice cream and candy toppings for fairies to taste, and lots of carnival rides and parties." She blushed when Dash raised her eyebrows. "I read all about the festival in the *Daily Scoop*," she confessed.

Dash smiled. "I know. I've read those articles too! The festival seems totally mint," she said. "And I've heard the Double Dip course is one of the most challenging sled races. The race is the last day of the festival."

"Does that mean you'll have to race against Menta and Peppa?" Minny asked. "They've been the champions for the past two years."

"So you know about those Mint Fairies?" Dash said, raising her eyebrows. "They make mint ice cream and live on Meringue Island. They definitely have an advantage because they've run the course so many times. But this year the race is going to be different."

"Why?" Minny asked, taking a sip of her drink.

"Because this year *I'm* in the race!" Dash boasted proudly. "I've never been to Mt. Ice Cream. But now that I've been invited to go, I can't wait! It's not every day that a fairy gets invited to race in Double Dip!" Dash's mind started to flood with ideas. "I can't wait to start working on a new sled. I'll need a double sled for this race," she explained. "And I know just the partner to pick to ride with me."

"Who?" Minny asked. She leaned in closer to Dash.

"The perfect fairy for the job," she said. "She's fearless, and she knows chocolate inside and out."

"Oh, I've read there is that chocolate-coated part of the course," Minny said. She tapped her finger on her head. "I've heard that is the part where lots of fairies fall off their sleds."

"Exactly!" Dash exclaimed. "So with my secret chocolate partner, I'll have the winning edge."

"And a good friend to race with," Minny said,

giggling. "I know you are talking about your friend Cocoa. She'll be fantastic."

Taking a bite of a mint, Dash nodded in agreement. "I hope that she agrees. We'd make a *sugar-tastic* team."

Dash called over another sugar fly. "I wonder if Carobee the dragon would take my friends and me to Meringue Island. The journey would be so sweet on top of a dragon! I hope he will agree to fly us across the Vanilla Sea." She wrote her note and handed it to the sugar fly. "You'll find Carobee in the caves on Meringue Island," Dash told the fly. "Please hurry, and wait for his reply!"

Dash imagined the green-and-purple dragon getting the sugar fly note. She and her friends had met Carobee when they'd been searching for gooey goblins. While they had been looking for the mischievous creatures, they'd found Carobee. The fairies had become fast friends with the dragon after that adventure. Dash hoped that Carobee would be part of this adventure too!

The fly buzzed off toward Meringue Island. Dash leaned back and took a deep, slow breath in and out. "I just know this is going to be my year to win," she said. "To win Double Dip is a huge honor."

"And to beat Menta and Peppa would be a great accomplishment," Minny added.

"Hmm," Dash said, closing her eyes, thinking about the moment of glory. "Can't you see Cocoa and me in the winner's circle?" She sighed. "This is going to be *so mint*!" she exclaimed. "But first I have to ask Cocoa to be my partner!"

CHAPTER 2

Sweet News

The sun was near the top of the Frosted Mountains when Dash arrived at Red Licorice Lake. She knew she was early for Sun Dip, but she was too excited—and maybe a little worried. Cocoa, her Chocolate Fairy friend, would be the best partner for her. But would she say yes to the race?

Dash knew that Cocoa liked adventures. She was a spunky fairy who had once stood up to Mogu the salty troll. He had stolen Cocoa's chocolate eggs, and she had gone all the way to Black Licorice Swamp to get them back. Cocoa was brave and clever. Even though Cocoa had never raced before, Dash knew that she had what it took to be a great speed racer.

Sitting down on the red sugar sand, Dash thought about what she would say to Cocoa. She spoke aloud, "Cocoa, I have the mintiest, most exciting quest . . . *Ach-hoo! Ach-hoo! Ach-hoo!*" Dash started sneezing, and then sniffled.

"Dash, are you all right?" Raina the Gummy Fairy asked as she landed next to her friend.

"Oh, yes, I'm fine," Dash said. "Nothing a little mint won't cure!" She reached into her pocket and showed off her new mint candy.

Raina smiled. "Your mint chips!" she exclaimed. "Those look delicious."

"And they taste good too," Dash said, grinning. "Try them." She poured some into Raina's hand.

"Mmm," Raina said. "Well done, Dash!"

"And that isn't the mint news of the day," Dash informed her.

"Tell me!" Raina said, moving closer.

Dash straightened up. She had planned on keeping her news a secret until all her friends had arrived, but she couldn't keep quiet any longer. She pulled her wings back and smiled at Raina. "I was invited to race in Double Dip!" she exclaimed.

Raina jumped up in the air. "Licking lollipops, Dash! That is *sugar-tastic*!"

"Do you think Cocoa will want to be my sledding partner?" Dash asked.

"Cocoa is one of the most fearless fairies," Raina said thoughtfully. "She could definitely help you out on the chocolate slope of the Double Dip course."

Dash flapped her wings enthusiastically. "Exactly. Plus, it sure would be so mint to race with a good friend." She looked at Raina. "Do you think that she'll say yes?"

"It's not even Sun Dip, and you are already eating and telling stories," Melli the Caramel Fairy said, interrupting their conversation. She smiled at her friends as she touched down on the ground.

Cocoa was right behind Melli. "Leave it to Dash to be early," she said. "And eating," she joked as she pointed to Dash's mint chips.

Raina laughed. "Something has gotten Dash all juiced up," she said. She faced Dash. "Tell them!" she whispered.

Dash grinned, and her silver wings fluttered. "Let's wait until Berry arrives," she said. "I want to share my news when everyone is here."

"That's not fair," Cocoa moaned. "You know Berry is *always* late."

Melli spread a blanket, and the four fairies sat

down. Dash saw that the sun was inching closer to the top of the mountains. She looked over toward Fruit Chew Meadow.

Please hurry, Berry! Dash thought. *For once, make it on time!*

Raina gave Dash a look. Dash wanted to ask Cocoa right then, but she thought it would be sweeter if all the fairies were together. She tapped her fingers on her knees. If Berry didn't arrive soon, Dash thought for sure she would burst!

"Ach-hoo! Ach-hoo! Ach-hoo!" Dash sneezed again. She noticed her friends sharing a look. "I'm fine," she told them. "Just some licorice pollen in the air, I'm sure."

Raina raised her eyebrows, but Dash jumped up and cut her off before she could say anything more. "There's Berry!" Dash cried, pointing up to the sky.

Berry floated down to her friends. The Fruit Fairy's red-and-pink dress was sparkling, and in her hair she wore matching sugarcoated barrettes. Berry loved fashion and was definitely the best-dressed fairy of the friends. Part of the reason she was often late was that she spent so much time getting ready.

"Hi, everyone!" Berry said. "Wait until you hear!" She grinned at all her friends. "I have the most delicious news!"

Raina put her hand up. "I don't know, Berry," she said, "Dash has something supersweet to share." She pushed Dash into the middle of the fairies.

"Tell us, Dash!" Melli said.

Dash grinned. "I was invited to be in the Double Dip race at Mt. Ice Cream during the Cone Harbor Festival!" she blurted out. She felt her cheeks flush with color as the excitement bubbled up inside her.

"Congratulations!" her friends all cheered.

"Wow," Melli said. "That is a great honor."

"Sweet strawberries," Berry said.

"I have another surprise, Cocoa," Dash said, turning to her. "I would love if you'd be my partner on the sled. Double Dip is a two-fairy race. I'd be honored if you'd race with me."

Cocoa's eyes sparkled. "One hundred and fifty cocoa percent!" she shouted. She shot up in the air and did a flip. "A race on Mt. Ice Cream? *Choc-o-licious!*"

"And Carobee is going to take us!" Dash said. "I sent a sugar fly message to him, and he wrote back right away. He can't wait to visit with us again."

"Sure as sugar, this is going to be such a great trip," Berry said. She grinned. "Your news is the icing on my news, Dash."

"What are you talking about?" Raina asked, eyeing her clever friend.

Berry stood up. "My delicious news is that Fruli has invited us all to stay at her place on Meringue Island for the Cone Harbor Festival weekend!"

"So mint!" Dash cheered. "Now we have a grand place to stay! Double Dip is the last event in the festival. This is scrumptious!"

"Fruli said we could all come?" Melli asked.

Berry nodded. "Yes, and that was before Dash and Cocoa were going to race! Now it's all even sweeter."

Fruli was a fancy Fruit Fairy from Meringue Island. She worked in Fruit Chew Meadow with Berry. There was a time when Berry had been very jealous of her, but now they were good friends.

Dash glanced up at the Frosted Mountains. The sun was nestled behind the high white peaks. She couldn't wait until the weekend, when Carobee would come fly them to Mt. Ice Cream. "This is going to be a trip to remember," she said, grinning.

3

Up, Up, and Away

Dash sat on the edge of the Gummy Forest dock, swinging her feet in the Vanilla Sea. She reached down and splashed her arms with the cool water. She sighed. Dash did not like waiting!

Squinting, Dash checked the sky. Not only was she waiting for her friends, she was also expecting Carobee. The green-and-purple dragon would be hard to miss! At one time Dash and her friends were afraid of him. Now they considered him a true friend.

Finally Melli and Cocoa arrived. They flew to the edge of the dock and sat down next to Dash.

"How are you feeling?" Melli asked. She peered closely at her minty friend. "Are you okay, Dash?"

"I'm fine, really," Dash said.

Cocoa looked more closely at her. "Are you sure? You don't look so well."

"And your voice is a little hoarse," Melli added.

Dash stood up. She coughed to clear her throat. "I'm fine. Today we're going to Mt. Ice Cream." She pointed out to the horizon. "*Nothing* is going to stop me from feeling good or going on this trip."

Raina laughed as she walked up the dock.

"I'd say that today is double-dip delicious," she said. "I am so excited to spend some time on Meringue Island." She pulled a notebook from her bag. "I've made a list of all the historical places that I would love to explore." Reaching into her bag again, she pulled out a thick book. "I've been reading up on the island, and there are so many cool sights."

"I know," Melli agreed. She moved closer to Raina. "Can I see that book? I was hoping to learn more about the Meringue Cliffs and the fairies who live there."

"Let's not forget that there's an ice cream festival," Cocoa said with a grin. "There will be lots of chocolate ice cream for me!"

"There are so many sites to see. I can't wait!" Melli said.

"Not to mention seeing Fruli's house," Cocoa added. "Berry thinks it's going to be gorgeous."

"Who cares about all that?" Dash said. She kept her eyes on the horizon. In the pale morning light she could barely make out the outline of Mt. Ice Cream. "Double Dip is one of the most challenging courses." She pointed to a crate at the end of the dock. "And I built an extraordinary sled. We're going to win!"

Cocoa held up her hand and Dash slapped a high five. "You can say that again, partner!" Cocoa said.

Dash stood up. "All I can think about is Double Dip," she said. "I can't wait to take first prize." She reached over and grabbed Cocoa's hand, raising it up in the air for a winning pose. "How do we look?" she asked.

"*So mint!*" Berry said as she flew in. "Is this the winning team of Double Dip?"

"Sure as sugar!" Dash and Cocoa said at the same time.

Raina started to laugh. "Berry, you know this is just a two-day trip, right?" She pointed to the large bags that Berry was holding in her hands.

"Those are two of the largest suitcases I've ever seen!" Melli gasped.

Berry laughed. "These cases are empty," she said, smiling. "I had to bring bags for all the clothes that I'm going to buy on Meringue Island!"

Dash rolled her eyes. "Of course," she said. "You are going to go to all of Fruli's favorite stores, right?"

Raising her eyebrows, Berry sighed. "I'm not sure I can afford all the stores where Fruli shops," she said. "Meringue Island has some of the fanciest stores in Sugar Valley. But I'm hoping to find some sweet deals."

"Or get some ideas for your own clothes," Melli said. "I think you're the best designer, Berry."

Berry blushed. "Thanks, Melli," she said. "I plan on buying lots of fabric."

"I hope that Carobee gets here soon," Dash said. She flew up in the air with her hand shielding her eyes, and then she started coughing nonstop.

"Dash, you sound awful!" Cocoa said.

Dash grabbed her throat. Her voice had sounded like a baby caramella bird's hoarse chirp.

"Oh, Dash," Raina said. "Your voice!"

Reaching into her backpack, Dash pulled out her thermos. She took a few sips of the liquid and cleared her throat. "There," she said, her voice sounding a little clearer. "Told you it was nothing that some soothing warm mint tea couldn't fix."

Her friends looked at her, unsure if Dash was really all right.

"Where is Carobee?" Dash continued. "I can't wait to get out on the slopes and take this sled for a spin. Right, Cocoa?"

Cocoa nodded, but she looked concerned. "Maybe you should just rest when we get to Fruli's," she said.

"Rest?" Dash snapped. "No way. There's too much to do today!" Then she pointed up to the sky. "And look, here comes Carobee!" Dash's heart began to race. Off in the distance she could see the immense span of Carobee's wings. Seeing her dragon friend made the journey to Double Dip very real! She waved her arms wildly and jumped up and down. "Over here, Carobee!" she cried. "We're ready for a winning adventure!"

CHAPTER 4

Sailing over the Sea

Carobee sailed down to the dock with his wide lavender wings. He gracefully bowed his head. "Hello," he greeted the fairies. "I am so happy to see all of you."

"And we are happy to see you," Dash said. She coughed a little, and then her face turned bright red. She couldn't stop coughing!

"Dash," Carobee said, "what's the matter? Are you okay?"

"Have some nectar," Raina said, holding out her bottle.

"That cough is getting worse," Melli muttered.

Dash fluttered her wings and flew over to her bag. Again she took out her thermos and gulped some warm mint tea. "I'll be fine," she finally managed to say. "It's not that bitter! I have my mint tea and mint drops."

"I know you always say that there's nothing mint can't cure," Melli said, "but your cough sounds terrible."

Raina stepped closer to her. "Maybe this trip isn't the best idea."

"I'm all right," Dash said firmly. "Please stop looking at me with those worried eyes!"

She wished her friends would stop staring at
her! Yes, her cough was a sour drip on the day,
but she wasn't going to let that spoil everything.
She just had to race in Double Dip! She wasn't

about to decline a great racing invitation—not for anything!

"Is everyone ready?" Dash asked in a much clearer voice. She took a deep breath, grateful that the tea had soothed her cough and that her voice sounded almost normal.

Berry took out long licorice ropes from one of her suitcases. "I thought that these would come in handy."

Dash was thankful that Berry had changed the subject. She grabbed one of the ropes and carefully draped the licorice around Carobee's neck.

"This is perfect," Dash told Berry. "Thank you for remembering to bring this licorice! It wouldn't be safe without a rope to hold on to as we flew."

"Remember how Mogu gave us those black

licorice ropes at Candy Castle for our journey across the Vanilla Sea?" Melli asked.

"Never would I have imagined that we'd use those ropes for flying on a dragon," Dash said, smiling at Carobee.

"I think that was the kindest thing Mogu has ever done for anyone," Cocoa said.

"Just proves how scared he was of the *gooey goblins!*" Melli said, giggling.

Dash glanced up at the sky. "Come on, everyone. We should get going," she said. "I want to get to Cone Harbor."

"Yes!" Cocoa cheered. "I can't wait to see the mounds of ice cream at the festival."

"And all those delicious toppings," Raina said, licking her lips. "I read in the *Daily Scoop* that this year there are even more candy toppings for the ice cream, grand parties, and even more rides than ever before. The crowds are supposed to be huge."

Melli took a newspaper from her backpack. "I have that article here!" she said. She unfolded the paper and then held it up to show her friends. "This festival is going to be the best ever."

Dash held up her hand. "Are we all forgetting about Double Dip? That is the real highlight," she said, grinning.

"Sure as sugar," Cocoa said, giving her friend a tight squeeze. "If we get in early enough, we should take a practice run."

Cocoa's idea made Dash smile. She knew that she had picked the right partner! Clearly, Cocoa understood the value of practice!

The friends climbed onto the dragon's back. They sat in a row, with Dash in the lead spot.

"How is Nillie?" Raina asked.

Nillie was the secret sea horse who ruled the Vanilla Sea. Dash scanned the sea below, looking for her. The fairies had once been frightened of Nillie, but the sea horse had proved to be a great friend and a huge help to them—just like Carobee.

"Would you like to say hello?" Carobee asked.

Before Dash could yank on the licorice rope to stop him, Carobee swooped down close to the sea. All Dash wanted to do was get out to the slopes of Double Dip. She wasn't interested in any detours!

The other fairies cheered loudly as they looked for the gentle sea horse. Two horselike heads surfaced near the water.

"Over there!" Cocoa called, pointing.

Carobee shifted to the left and got closer to

the sea. "Hello, Sprinkle and Bean!" the dragon roared.

Nillie's twins, who guarded the sea, surfaced. They were surprised to see the Candy Fairies on the dragon's back.

"Everything all right?" Bean asked.

"Yes!" Dash replied. "We're off to the Cone Harbor Festival. Cocoa and I are racing in Double Dip."

Sprinkle jumped up and did a double flip. "Good luck," he cheered.

"Stop by on your trip home," Bean called as Carobee lifted higher up, away from the water.

"We'll come show you our medals!" Cocoa said. She smiled at Dash. "Our first-place medals!"

Dash was happy that Cocoa was excited. She admired her spirit and her positive outlook. She flashed Cocoa a smile. "We'll be the sweetest team ever," she said.

"*Choc-o-rific!*" Cocoa cheered.

"Wow," Dash said, peering over Carobee's wing. The view from the dragon's back was spectacular. Being up so high, the fairies could see all of Sugar Valley and the clear waters of the Vanilla Sea. They all settled down for a smooth ride high in the clouds. The sea seemed to stretch out forever. Soon Dash spotted Rock Candy Isle and knew that it wouldn't be too long until they saw the peaks of Meringue Island.

"Look over there," Melli said, pointing down below. "I see Cone Harbor!"

Carobee was heading straight for the shores of Meringue Island. Even from far away, they could see there were heaps of ice cream in large buckets and a wide assortment of candy on display.

"Licking lollipops," Berry gasped. "Look at all the Candy Fairies who are here."

Dash surveyed the scene below. Berry was right. Candy Fairies from all over Sugar Valley crowded the beach to take part in the beginning of the festival. Dash's wings tingled as she watched from Carobee's back. And then her nose began to itch. She didn't want to sneeze again and worry her friends, so she tried to stifle her sneeze. Luckily, her friends were so drawn into the scene in the harbor that no one noticed.

"Look at those carnival rides!" Melli shouted.

"And all that ice cream," Cocoa said, her eyes wide.

"I wish this festival was longer than just a weekend," Raina added.

Carobee touched down on the sugar sand. "Here you are," he said. "Welcome to Meringue Island!"

"The sweetest words ever!" Berry exclaimed. "And look, there's Fruli!" She spotted her glamorous friend in the crowd and jumped off Carobee's back.

"I've never seen Berry move so fast," Raina joked.

"She has a plan," Dash said. "Just like me." She winked at Cocoa. "Only I don't plan to be flying around stores. I'll be flying down the Double Dip course!"

Melli nudged Cocoa's arm and nodded.

"What?" Dash asked.

"We think that maybe it would be a good idea for you to go back to Fruli's house to rest,"

Cocoa said. "It was a long ride from Gummy Forest, so we should just take it easy."

"Rest?" Dash asked. "Are you kidding? We've got to get in a practice run!" As she started to get excited her voice gave out, and she started coughing once again.

Cocoa put her arm around Dash. "We'll run the course in the morning. It's been a long day." She handed Dash her thermos of hot peppermint tea.

Dash took some tea and then followed her friends over to see Fruli.

Maybe a good night's sleep would help my cough, she thought.

Though she wasn't sure how she was going to sleep! Being so close to Mt. Ice Cream was making her anything but tired!

CHAPTER

5

Sweet Home

Welcome to Meringue Island!" Fruli cried, greeting her friends. "How was your trip here?"

"A smooth ride," Dash said, grinning. "Thanks to Carobee."

Fruli waved at the green-and-purple dragon over by the shore. Then she turned to her friends. "Come on," she said. "There are going to be lots of celebrations tonight. This year's festival is going to be the biggest yet!"

"Are there many racers for Double Dip?" Dash asked.

Berry laughed. "Dash has a one-track mind," she said to Fruli.

"And it's the fast track!" Cocoa added. "Dash and I are going to race together."

Fruli nodded. "Yes, Berry told me. You will have some tough competition," she said. "Menta and Peppa are racing again this year. They have won the past two years in a row."

"Yes, we know," Dash said, looking around at all the fairies in the harbor.

"Menta is a little pushy," Fruli said. "And her sister, Peppa, is not much nicer. They have a reputation for fighting all the time, but they *are* fantastic racers."

Dash didn't want to admit it, but she was a little worried. The sisters would be hard to beat since they knew the course so well. It was very challenging—lots of double dips, and that slick chocolate slope. But Dash would have a Chocolate Fairy with her. She hoped that key ingredient in her plan would help win the race.

"I know about the mint sisters," Dash told Fruli. "But Cocoa and I are . . ." Her hoarse voice trailed off into a deep, barking cough.

"We are going to win," Cocoa finished for her. She handed Dash her thermos. "Here, Dash, drink some more. And maybe try not talking."

"That's not going to be easy for Dash," Melli

said. "But I bet resting your voice will help."

Fruli shook her head. "Oh, Dash," she said. "I'm so sorry you are sick."

"I'm not sick," Dash replied. Only this time, hardly any sound came out of her mouth when she spoke. Her blue eyes widened.

Why is this happening? she thought. *Why now?*

Cocoa took the thermos from Dash. "Don't worry," she said. "You'll get some rest tonight. We have another day before the race."

Dash wasn't sure what to think. She felt so tired, but she wanted—and needed—to practice. Her head was beginning to spin, so she followed her friend towards Fruli's house. As they flew over Cone Harbor they saw fairies setting up decorations for the start of the festival. There were colorful banners all along the harbor. Not everyone was all about the Double Dip race. There were many fairies in the harbor for the ice cream and the festive parties.

Up ahead, Dash saw meringue peaks and beautiful cloth canopies swaying in the breeze. Fruli's home looked like a castle!

All the fairies landed on the large terrace on the second floor and went inside. Berry turned around in a circle.

"Sweet strawberries!" Berry exclaimed. "This house is gorgeous!"

Fruli blushed. "This house has been in my family for a long time," she explained. "My great-grandparents built this place many years ago."

"They did a *sweet-tacular* job," Raina said, looking around. "There are so many details, and this fabric is delicious!" She touched one of the many lounge chairs.

"Everything is grown or made here on Meringue Island," Fruli said. "Please make your-selves comfortable. There are beds set up here in this room. I thought you would all like to stay together."

"Thank you," Berry said, speaking for her friends. "This is just perfect."

"Tonight we're hosting the Dip Party at our house. You are all invited to come," Fruli said. "I am going to change and then go downstairs to help."

Berry lugged her suitcase into the room. "Oh, I have a special outfit for tonight!" she exclaimed. "I sewed rainbow sprinkles onto my dress." She pulled the colorful dress out of her suitcase.

Dash stepped into the large bedroom. There were five beds with canopies draped over each one and thick comforters made of the softest cotton candy. Dash couldn't help but want to snuggle into a bed.

"Maybe I'll take a little rest before dinner," Dash said.

"That sounds like a good idea," Cocoa agreed. She put Dash's thermos next to her bed. "We'll wake you when we head downstairs."

Dash put her head down on the smooth pillow and in an instant was fast asleep. Thoughts of sledding filled her head, and she slept peacefully.

6

A Minty Mess

Dash rolled over and opened one eye. For a second she didn't know where she was, and she quickly sat up. Cocoa was standing near her bed, peering down at her.

"Everyone!" Cocoa called over her shoulder. "She's up!" She sat down on the edge of the bed and looked over at Dash. "How do you feel?"

Rubbing her eyes, Dash leaned back on the soft pillows. She pulled the blanket up to her chin. And then she started to cough.

"That is a salty cough," Raina said, coming over to the bed. She handed Dash a large mug. "I just made you a fresh pot of peppermint tea. I hope this helps your throat."

Dash was grateful for the warm liquid and drank the whole mug before trying to speak. She looked behind Raina and Cocoa at the window on the far side of the room. Sunlight was streaming in and casting a bright light.

How can that be? Dash thought. *We got here before Sun Dip. What time is it?*

"You fell asleep last night," Cocoa told her. "We thought we'd let you sleep so you would feel better."

"You fell asleep in a second," Raina told her.

"And you didn't move all night," Melli added.

"Dash, you missed the Dip Party downstairs," Berry said, coming closer to the bed. "It was truly *sugar-tacular*! There were the most amazing candies, and the ice cream was delicious. And you should have seen Fruli's new dress. It was made of—"

Melli tugged at Berry's arm. Dash could tell that she was trying to get Berry to cool down on the descriptions of everything she'd missed last night. Berry was all juiced up about the grand party. The truth was, Dash didn't really care. She only wanted to head out to the slopes and try out her new double-dip sled.

"Sorry, Dash," Berry said softly. "I really missed you."

Dash smiled. "It's okay. I'm glad that you had fun."

"So, how do you feel now?" Cocoa asked. "I already waxed the sled with frosting. I know that you wanted to try to take a practice run this morning."

Melli gave Cocoa a hard look. "Do you think that is a good idea?" she asked.

Throwing off the covers, Dash leaped out of bed. "Sounds like a pure mint plan," she said.

"That peppermint tea did the trick, right?" Raina asked with a sly grin.

"You bet your peppermint leaves," Dash said.

Shaking her head, Melli looked concerned. "I'm not so sure about this," she said. "Dash, maybe you should stay in today, or at least this morning."

"The race is tomorrow," Dash said. She reached for her boots and slipped them on. "Cocoa and I have to try out the sled today. If there are any adjustments we need, we can make them tonight."

Berry handed Dash a small bag. "Take some

of these fruit chews," she told her. "I know the peppermint tea is helping your throat, but these chews should help you too."

"I need all the help I can get," Dash said. "Thanks, Berry." She turned to Cocoa. "Are you ready?"

"Sure as sugar!" Cocoa exclaimed. "We'll meet you in Cone Harbor for lunch," she said to her friends. "Berry, remember, you only have two suitcases!"

"Very funny," Berry said. "I plan to do lots of shopping, don't you worry!"

"And we're going to do some sightseeing," Raina said, smiling at Melli.

Dash laughed. "Sounds like we all have a plan for the day."

✦ ✦ ✦

Dash and Cocoa flew to Mt. Ice Cream and were surprised to find many fairy racers. The slopes were filled with fairies on double sleds trying out the icy slopes.

At the top of the mountain there was a large sign with a map of the trails. Double Dip was a five-sugar-cube-level course. This was the highest level in Sugar Valley. Dash noticed that Cocoa looked a little nervous.

"I know you haven't raced a course like this one," she said. "But don't worry, I'll help you out."

Cocoa pointed to the map. "I'm not sure about this part over here," she said. "I didn't realize that it's a *solid* chocolate area." She tilted her head as she thought through the problem. "Maybe we should try something different in that spot."

"What?" Dash said, not really listening. Her attention was focused on the starting line. Menta and Peppa were getting into their sleek new sugarcoated sled.

"Dash, are you listening to me?" Cocoa asked.

Turning her attention back to Cocoa, Dash pulled her goggles on. "Let's go check out the slope."

"But we need to have a race plan," Cocoa said. "If we know the slippery chocolate is coming up, we'll need to change our speed."

But Dash didn't hear a word—she was already flying toward the lineup. Cocoa shrugged and followed her.

At the starting line Dash jumped into the front of her sled. "Cocoa, since you're taller, you need to sit in the rear. You take the back."

Cocoa slipped into the sled and settled into her seat. She pulled her goggles over her eyes.

Dash couldn't help overhearing Peppa and Menta next to them. The sisters were screaming at each other!

"How green can you be?" barked Menta. She was glaring at her sister as Dash and Cocoa readied their sled for the run. "There is no way you can steer through that course without *me* telling *you* what to do."

Dash watched Peppa's face get redder and her eyes narrow at her sister. Peppa twisted her long hair up into a bun and then took a deep breath. "You are one to talk," she barked. "You almost took off the back blade on that last run. You need to listen to *me* out on the slope. I know what I'm doing."

"And I know what I am doing!" Menta argued back.

Dash glanced over at Cocoa. The rumors about the fighting sisters were true. And Dash could see why. The fairies were different in every way imaginable. Peppa had blond hair and was tall and thin. Menta had dark hair and was much shorter and wider. Dash wondered how they managed to win so many races with all their bickering.

"So these are the champions?" Cocoa whispered.

"Yes," Dash said. She watched as they took off down the slope. They sailed around the first turn, and then they were gone. "They always manage to win."

"Well, not this year!" Cocoa said, trying to sound enthusiastic.

The two friends began their practice run. They sled through the first part of the course. Dash was yelling instructions to Cocoa and kept a close watch on their time. Feeling pleased with their run, Dash smiled to herself.

This is going to be a smooth race, she thought.

On the approaching turn to the chocolate slope, the sled began to slip. Dash held on tight.

"It's the chocolate!" Cocoa shouted over the rushing wind. "We need to slow down as we make the turn!"

"But we'll lose time," Dash said anxiously. She leaned back to speak to Cocoa. She couldn't turn around. She had to keep her eyes on the course. "We can't slow down!" she shouted. "I know what I'm doing!"

"Cold chocolate gets very slick," Cocoa

advised. "This part of the slope is dangerous."

Dash tried to respond, but no sound came out of her mouth. Her yelling made her throat tickle, and then the coughing started again. As she coughed she lost control of the sled. The sled rammed into a scoop of chocolate fudge swirl.

Cocoa jumped out of the sled. "What are you doing?" she barked. "You can't just turn off the course like that!" Then Cocoa realized Dash had crashed because of her coughing.

Quickly Cocoa gave her friend the thermos. Only this time, the tea didn't soothe the cough. Dash's whole face was red, and her eyes were filled with tears.

Dash felt woozy. There was no denying the fact that she was sick. And now the sled was damaged. This was a giant minty mess.

CHAPTER

7

Double Mint Mistake

Dash was still coughing and showing no sign of stopping.

In her pocket Dash found the fruit chews that Berry had given her. She started to suck on the treats, and her throat began to feel better. At least she could stop coughing! She flew out of the sled and checked the damage to the front blades.

Dash looked down at the ground. First no voice and now no sled. Things were looking pretty bitter.

"What's going on?" Raina called out. She flew up to her friends with Berry and Melli close behind. "We were just coming to see how you were doing."

Melli examined the damaged sled. "Are you all right?" she asked. "Looks like a bad crash."

Cocoa stood up and flapped her wings. "We're fine," she said. "I'm not so sure about the sled, though." She knelt down and looked at the bent front blades. "But we need to get Dash back to Fruli's house. She doesn't have a voice at all now. And she nearly got us buried in ice cream because she couldn't stop barking orders—or coughing!"

Dash wanted to answer, but she found she still couldn't speak at all. She stuck her lip out.

Of all the minty things to go wrong, she thought. *This is a bitter disaster!*

"Let's get you both back to Fruli's," Berry said. "Raina and I will take the sled. I'm sure we can fix it up."

Dash's head was swirling too fast to argue about anything else. The thought of lying in that cozy, soft bed at Fruli's house was so appealing to her. She wanted to close her eyes and forget about her fight with Cocoa, the crash, and the damaged sled.

Back at Fruli's house, Dash climbed into bed. Melli puffed up the pillows so that she wouldn't cough so much when she put her head down.

Fruli took Dash's temperature and shook her head. "It's official," she said. "Dash is sick."

Dash was miserable. All she could do was close her eyes. Before she drifted off to sleep, she overheard Cocoa and Melli talking.

"She was supersalty," Cocoa told Melli. "Maybe I was being a little too strong-willed on the chocolate slope, but Dash wasn't listening to me at all."

"What do you mean?" Melli asked. "You are a Chocolate Fairy! If anyone knows chocolate, it's you!"

"Dash is the experienced rider," Cocoa said. "Only she was so minty! She kept yelling at me the whole time."

"Sometimes Dash is a little too fast for her own good," Raina added.

Dash was *still* bitter. How could Cocoa say that about her? She turned over and faced the wall. And since she couldn't tell anyone how she felt, she fell into a deep sleep.

When Dash woke up, she was surprised to find Berry sitting by her side, sewing a beautiful pink-and-orange fabric. Dash guessed that it was a new purchase from the morning's shopping spree.

"Hi, Dash," Berry said brightly. "Have some ice cream shake. It is so delicious." She handed her a tall glass with a pink straw. "I'm sure the cold ice cream will feel good on your sore throat."

Berry was right, and Dash enjoyed the soothing cold drink. She sat up and looked around the empty room. She was sure that Berry would rather be out shopping.

She tried to talk, but still no words came out. Berry reached for a pad of paper and a pen and handed them to Dash. "Kinda like sending a sugar fly message without the fly!" Berry joked.

Dash quickly wrote out her message and handed the pad to Berry.

Berry laughed. "Oh, Dash," she said. "I can always go shopping! But I came to see you race Double Dip, and you are going to get better for the race."

Dash stared out the window at Mt. Ice Cream. The view from the window was extraordinary, and she could even see the Double Dip course. There were some sleds on the mountain, and Dash felt a lump in her stomach. Without

practice time, she and Cocoa would be at a huge
disadvantage. She hung her head.

Who am I kidding? Dash thought. *Cocoa is so
angry at me. She probably doesn't even want to race
with me anymore.*

"Cheer up," Berry said.

Dash took the pad of paper and wrote another
note. She handed the paper to Berry.

"Yes," she said. "Cocoa is with Raina and Fruli."

Dash walked out to the balcony and sank down onto one of the lounge chairs. Cone Harbor Festival happened once a year. Of all the times for her to feel sick—and to be fighting with her friend! This was a doubly minty mistake.

Berry came and sat down at the foot of her bed. "Don't feel so sad," she said. "Fruli and the others will be back."

All Dash knew was that being sick and angry was not a good combination. She closed her eyes and hoped that she would be feeling better soon.

CHAPTER

8

A Sweeter Way

Dash spent the afternoon sitting on the balcony at Fruli's house. She still wasn't able to speak, and her throat felt very sore. Being sick and away from home was not fun, but at least here she could still look out and see Mt. Ice Cream. Dash couldn't take her eyes off the action on the slopes. There were many sleds racing down the mountain. She wished that she could be taking practice runs too.

If only I had a racing partner and *a sled,* she thought sadly.

Dash sank down lower in the chair.

"Do you want anything?" Berry asked. All afternoon Berry had kept asking her if she wanted anything. Berry's being sweet to her wasn't helping Dash's mood at all.

"You have to try these meringue cookies," Berry said. She held out a plate to Dash. When Dash refused, Berry shook her head. "It's not like you to turn down a snack."

Dash didn't feel like eating. In fact, she didn't feel like doing anything.

"Hi, Dash!" Melli called from above. She flew down and landed next to Dash's lounge

chair. "Guess what? I was able to find some extra-gooey caramel to fix your sled. It will be as good as new now." She held out a pail of golden syrup.

Dash reached over for her pad of paper. She quickly wrote a note to Melli and handed it to her.

"You're welcome," Melli said after she read the note. "And yes, I do think that you'll be able to race tomorrow." Then she turned to Berry. "Have Fruli, Raina, and Cocoa come back yet?"

"No," Berry said. "Not yet."

Melli smiled at Dash. "Do you feel better?"

Wishing that she did feel better, Dash shook her head. This day was not turning out how she had planned.

Berry pointed up to the sky. "Look, here they come!" she said.

Dash sat up and saw Fruli leading Raina and Cocoa to the balcony. Fruli was holding a small rectangular box. She imagined that her friends had all had a great time—even without her.

"Hi, Dash!" Raina said. "I'm glad to see you sitting out here."

With a little shrug, Dash nodded. She didn't take her eyes off the small white box in Fruli's hands.

"Mission complete?" Berry asked.

"Sure as sugar," Cocoa gloated.

Dash wondered what her friends were talking about.

Raina sat down on a chair next to Dash. "After you fell asleep last night, I was reading through the Fairy Code Book," Raina told her. "I read a story about a Candy Fairy who had a bad sore throat. As I was reading to everyone Fruli remembered the story too."

"She remembered about the ice cream sandwiches!" Cocoa blurted out. "And I made the chocolate cookie part of the treat."

Dash faced Cocoa. She couldn't believe Cocoa was talking to her and that she had gone to all the trouble of making her a healing treat. Her friends hadn't been just out celebrating at the festival.

"I felt bad about our fight, Dash," Cocoa said, moving closer to her. "I was stubborn too. And then with you getting sick, I knew that I had to do something. I hope this works."

Fruli stepped forward. "The ice cream from the far side of the mountain is known to have healing powers," she said. "With Cocoa's help,

we made these mini mint-chip ice cream sand-wiches."

"Go ahead," Cocoa said. "Try one."

Fruli opened the box. In three neat rows were twelve mini round sandwiches. Dash didn't know what to say. She picked one up and took a bite. The rich chocolate outside went so nicely with the minty ice cream. Dash closed her eyes as the cold ice cream slid down her sore throat.

"So mint," Dash said. Her eyes grew wider. Her voice was back!

"Well, that was fast!" Melli said, grinning.

"Do you feel different?" Raina asked, leaning forward.

Dash reached for another mini ice cream sandwich. "I'll have another one to be sure," she said brightly.

"The mint ice cream remedy has helped fairies on the island for centuries," Fruli explained.

Pulling out the Fairy Code Book, Raina flipped to the chapter about the healing ice cream. "See?" she said. "Here is the story about those healing ice cream sandwiches. I'm so glad that I stumbled upon the story last night. And that Fruli knew just where to find the ice cream!"

"Thank you," Dash said. "Thank you to all of you for being so sweet to me. I know that I've been a bit minty."

"We understand," Berry said. "No one likes being sick."

"Especially the day before a big race," Melli added.

Dash groaned. "I can't believe the race is tomorrow."

Raina pulled a map from her bag. "Maybe this will help?" she said. "I got this from a booth near the starting line. It's the whole course. I know it's not the same as actually racing, but you and Cocoa can study the route and come up with a good strategy for the race. This map shows all the trails and toppings along the way."

"And with the caramel that Melli got today, I can fix the sled," Cocoa told Dash. She squeezed Dash's hand. "Please say that you'll do this. I want to make this happen. I really want to win."

"Sure as sugar," Dash said. She sat up and studied the map.

"Teamwork is always the fastest way to the finish line," Melli said.

"And Peppa and Menta don't have that going for them at all!" Cocoa exclaimed. "You should have heard them today in town."

"It was hard for anyone not to hear them," Fruli said. "They were screaming at each other from one store or booth to another!"

"Those two will never cross the finish line," Berry said, shaking her head.

Dash had to agree. And she was grateful for Raina's clever thinking. If they couldn't be on the slopes, the next best thing was to at least *study* the slopes!

Together, Dash and Cocoa talked over the

course using a sugar hair clasp from Berry's collection as the sled. Melli wrote down what they said so that they could have a record to help them remember the plan for the race.

"We might have a chance," Dash said.

"We have a double-good chance!" Cocoa said with a smile. "I'm glad we're not fighting anymore."

"Me too," Dash said, grinning. "It's much sweeter this way!"

9

Green as Mint

That night, instead of heading down to the harbor, the fairies stayed at Fruli's house. They all thought Dash needed one more night of rest, and no one wanted to leave her.

"We can watch the fireworks from the balcony," Fruli said. "When I was a little fairy, I used to watch from this spot. We have a good view of Cone Harbor. We can have a picnic out here and avoid all the crowds."

"Sounds delicious to me," Berry said happily.

"I can't wait," Melli added.

Dash was glad that her friends wanted to be with her. And she was very happy to be feeling healthier.

True to Fruli's word, the view was perfect. The fairies felt as if they had front-row seats for the colorful fireworks.

"The fireworks are *sugar-tastic!*" Melli said, enjoying the special seats.

"We appreciate you having us all," Raina told her.

"I'm happy you could all be here," Fruli replied. "And I'm very glad that Dash is feeling better. I can't wait for the race tomorrow."

"Me neither!" Dash and Cocoa said at the same time.

Right before the lights were turned out for the night, Dash gathered her friends together on her bed. "Your trip to Meringue Island isn't what you had planned," she said sadly. "Berry, your shopping time was cut short. And Raina and Melli, you didn't get lots of sightseeing done."

"I did eat lots of chocolate ice cream," Cocoa said, rubbing her belly.

Dash hung her head. "Berry, it wasn't fair you had to stay in all day with me, and the rest of you worked so hard on those ice cream sandwiches and fixing the sled."

"Fair?" Berry asked, raising her dark eyebrows up high. "Fair, fair, lemon square. You would have done the same for each of us. I'm just so happy to hear your voice again!" She walked over to her bed and pulled out a bag that she had put underneath the cotton-candy blanket. "And now for my surprise!" she declared. She held up two sparkling pink and orange sledding outfits. "I made you and Cocoa matching racing suits!"

Dash laughed. "Berry, those are *so mint!*"

Berry grinned. "I was hoping you'd say that!"

"Now get some rest so you'll be perfect for the race," Cocoa ordered. She gave her friend a tight squeeze. "Sweet dreams."

Curling up in her pink bed, Dash fell off to sleep. She had the best friends in the whole world. She couldn't wait for the sun to rise and for the race day to begin. With her friends beside her, she was ready for whatever happened.

The next morning, Dash's fever was gone. When she opened her eyes, she felt minty fresh. She sprang out of bed and went out to the balcony, where she found Cocoa already dressed and ready for the day. She was carefully inspecting the sled.

"Good morning," Cocoa said when she saw Dash. "How are you feeling?"

"Fresh as a new mint leaf," Dash boasted. "Those ice cream sandwiches were the perfect healing treat."

Cocoa smiled. "I knew that you'd be fine for today. The sled looks perfect, don't you think?"

Dash leaned down and checked the sled. She had to admit that Cocoa and Melli had done a fine job of mending the front blades.

"Sweet sugar," Dash said, "this is a winner!"

"I added this chocolate bar in the back to steady the sled a little bit," Cocoa said. She pointed to the addition on the end. "What do you think?"

Dash surveyed the change. "I'd say that having a Chocolate Fairy as a teammate was the smartest choice I could have made," she replied. "I never would have thought of that and I know that it will help over the slick chocolate part of the course."

Cocoa stood up with her chest puffed out proudly. "Aw, sweet chips," she said. "Thanks. I hope this all works out."

"Are mint leaves green?" Dash exclaimed. "This sled is made for first place." She stood tall.

"And this win will be even sweeter because we'll win the race together."

The two fairies hugged. Dash knew that fighting with a friend was salty business but making up was the sweetest part.

"Come on," she said to her sledmate. "Let's get going."

The two fairies quickly ate their breakfast and headed to the top of Mt. Ice Cream. There were many fairy teams lined up ready to race, and the grandstands were full of cheering fairies. Cocoa looked nervous.

"Don't worry," Dash said. "We're going to follow our plan." She looked Cocoa in the eye. "I trust you. And you trust me."

Cocoa smiled. "One hundred and fifty chocolate percent!" she said, grinning.

To the left of them, Peppa and Menta were pulling up their sled. Dash noticed that theirs was the newest model in the Sweet Slider 5000 series—the most expensive sled on the market. But she held her head high. She knew that her sled had been made with careful thought.

"Don't pull that," Peppa barked at her sister. She flipped her blond hair over to one side.

"It's fine," growled Menta.

Dash and Cocoa nodded to each other. Melli was right. If those two kept fighting, surely they would lose.

Even though the sisters were wearing matching outfits, they were definitely not racing the same race. They couldn't even agree on where to leave their sled while they signed in at the judges' table!

The giant clock clanged, and all riders were called to the official starting line.

Dash spotted their friends in the stands. It was hard to miss Berry in her new colorful outfit.

"I guess Berry did get to shop this morning," Dash whispered to Cocoa.

"She's dressed to win," Cocoa said. "So let the races begin!"

As all the sleds lined up, Dash felt the tension growing. Everyone there wanted to take home first prize. She looked back at Cocoa. "Are you ready?" she asked, pulling down her snow goggles.

"You bet your chocolate chips I am!" Cocoa said.

TWEEEEEET! The starting whistle blew!

"Then let's win this race!" Dash shouted.

10

Double Sweet

As the cold air pushed against Dash's face, she smiled. She had dreamt of this moment for a long time. Being out on the slopes of Mt. Ice Cream felt incredible! Yesterday she didn't think that she'd be able to feel the speed of sledding down the slick, icy slopes.

"Holy peppermint!" Dash screamed. "Here we go!"

All around her were double sleds with determined fairies. She tried to stay focused and gripped her wheel tightly. There was nothing like the rush of a fast race downhill.

"First turn, coming up," Cocoa said from behind.

Even though the pair had not run the entire course, they both felt that they knew all the curves and dips of the mountain. By studying the map, they had prepared themselves well. Dash kept her legs straight heading into the curve, knowing that a sharp left was coming up.

"Sweet syrup!" Dash cried as their sled pulled ahead of five others. If all the Mint Fairies in

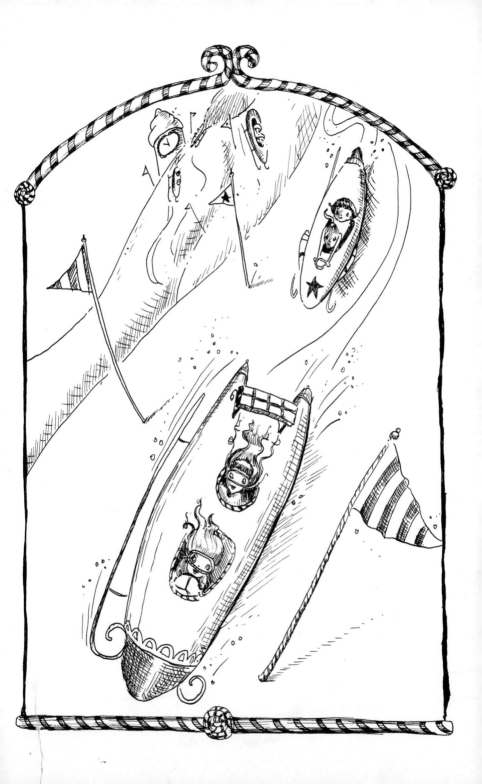

Sugar Valley could see her now! She thought of Minny and how excited she'd be when she heard all about Dash's adventure.

And maybe I'll be able to show her the shiny first-place medal, Dash thought.

She squinted and stared at the trail ahead. If they were going to win, she had to focus on the race, not the prize!

A few yards ahead of their sled, Dash spotted Menta and Peppa. It was hard to miss their bright green outfits and cotton-candy-pink sled. Dash wondered if they spent as much time picking out their outfits as they did on the slopes. Her heart beat faster, and she had to slow her breath with deep inhales and exhales. Now was the tricky part of the course—the chocolate topping section of the mountain. She had to stay clear headed!

"You all right?" Dash called back.

"Yes," Cocoa shouted over the wind. "Here comes the chocolate!"

As they closed in on Menta and Peppa, Dash could hear them fighting.

"Stay the course!" Dash called back as they headed toward the slick, hard chocolate.

"Slow down," Cocoa said. "We have to take this curve slowly."

Dash's instinct was to push forward, but she remembered what had happened during their practice run. This time she listened to her Chocolate Fairy friend. The extra chocolate weight in the back of the sled helped them steady the sled on the turn. Dash was grateful for Cocoa's clever chocolate planning. They rounded the bend and sailed past Peppa and Menta!

"Who was that?" Peppa snapped as Dash and Cocoa sped by.

Sure as sugar, their plan had worked!

The finish line was straight ahead. Dash couldn't believe they were so close. She wasn't sure if Peppa and Menta were behind or next to them. Dash squeezed the wheel and held tight as the sled soared ahead.

Down the mountain they sped. Dash felt the finish-line ribbon break as the sled crossed over the cherry-red stripe drizzled on the ice.

"Sweet chocolate chips!" Cocoa cheered. "Dash, we did it!"

In a flash their friends surrounded their sled. There was lots of hugging and cheering. Dash reached out to Cocoa.

"Winning has never been so sweet!" she said.

Princess Lolli, the gentle and kind ruler of Sugar Valley, flew over to the winners. "Congratulations," she said, beaming with pride. "You were *sugar-tastic* out there. Well done."

"Thank you," Dash and Cocoa said together.

"Come," Princess Lolli said. She was holding two shiny sugarcoated medals in her hand. "Fly with me over to the winner's circle. We need to present the two of you with your first-place prize."

Dash was overwhelmed by all the attention. There were so many fairies! She gripped Cocoa's hand. She was glad her friend was with her.

The *Daily Scoop* had a few reporters taking interviews and photographs.

"Congratulations," a reporter with orange wings called out. She was holding a notepad in her hand. "Please tell me your names."

"Dash and Cocoa," Dash proudly told her.

"How does it feel to win Double Dip?" she asked.

"Sweet as sugar!" Dash replied.

Dash spotted Menta and Peppa off to the side. They weren't arguing anymore. For the first time, they were speechless. Dash felt sorry for them. She knew that losing a race didn't feel good at all.

"We had some great competition out there," Dash went on to say. "It was a tough race. Everyone out there did a great job. And I'd like to thank my sledmate, Cocoa. She is a true friend and a dedicated racer."

The crowd cheered, and Cocoa gave Dash a tight squeeze.

"I owe so much to Dash," Cocoa said into the microphone. "She taught me everything!"

Princess Lolli slipped the medals over the winners' heads and posed with them for a picture for the paper. Then she turned to the crowd. "Who's ready for some treats?"

The crowd roared in response and moved toward the harbor.

"Oh, this is my favorite part of the festival," Fruli said as she reached Dash and Cocoa. "And the winner of the race gets to make the first double dip."

"What is a double dip?" Dash asked.

"It's an ice-cream cone that you dip in two toppings. You can't just have one, there are so many toppings at the festival!"

Dash checked out all the barrels lined up on

the stage. "Everything is always better with a touch of mint," she said with a grin. She dipped her cone in mint and then in mini chocolate chips. "To honor two great tastes and teammates!"

Everyone laughed, and Cocoa held out her cone. "Hit me with some mint too," she said.

Dash happily dipped Cocoa's cone. Sure, friends argue, but the sweetest part of friendship is making up. This certainly was a double-dip celebration!

FIND OUT

WHAT HAPPENS IN

T he sun shone down on the Royal Gardens at Candy Castle. Berry the Fruit Fairy sat under a lollipop tree with her friend Raina, a Gummy Fairy. "It feels like everyone in Candy Kingdom is outside today," Berry said.

"On a day like this, it's hard to stay inside,"

Raina replied. She tilted her face up toward the sun's rays.

Berry smiled. It was the first warm day of spring, and all the fairies in Sugar Valley were buzzing around. After the chilly winter, the warm sunshine was a welcome feeling.

"Thanks for meeting me for lunch today," Berry told her. "I'm sorry I missed Sun Dip last night."

Sun Dip was a time when Candy Fairies gathered to talk about their day. During the last moments of daylight, Candy Fairies shared stories and sweet treats. Yesterday Berry had missed out on seeing her group of friends.

"Did you finish planting the jelly bean seedlings?" Raina asked.

Berry's wings fluttered. "Yes," she said. "I

needed the extra time last night. The seedlings are getting so tall, so I planted them all."

"Princess Lolli is going to love the new crop of jelly beans," Raina said, smiling. "Our basket is going to be *sugar-tastic!*"

Berry and her friends were making a special basket for Princess Lolli's upcoming journey to see her sister, Princess Sprinkle. Princess Sprinkle lived on Cupcake Lake and ruled over Cake Kingdom. Each sister brought the other the best of her kingdom's crops to share when she visited.

On her last visit, Princess Sprinkle brought beautiful cupcakes, cakes, cookies, and brownies. The Cake Fairies were known for their tasty treats. The Candy Fairies always had a feast during those visits. For Princess Lolli's trip,

Berry had wanted to give the fairies in Cake Kingdom a special sweet treat of her own.

"Cocoa and Melli showed us the basket last night," Raina said. "They worked very hard and it is beautiful."

"And did Dash find the nighttime mints?" Berry asked. "I know she was worried about getting the right size mint for Princess Lolli to see in the Forest of Lost Flavors."

Raina shivered. "Oh, I don't like thinking of that place," she said. "All those white, flavorless trees . . ." Her voice trailed off.

Berry had heard many stories about the creepy forest from Raina. The Gummy Fairy loved books and owned the largest collection in Sugar Valley. There was plenty written about the Forest of Lost Flavors. The wide area split the land between Candy Kingdom and Cake Kingdom. Most Candy Fairies stayed far away from the eerie forest. Nothing grew there anymore—no candy crops at all. Now there were just tall white trees without any flavor. That forest was not somewhere you'd want to be without any light, and it was scariest at night.

"I am sure Princess Lolli is going to love our basket," Berry said. "It is an honor to make her one for her trip. I don't remember the last time she went to see her sister."

"Princess Sprinkle has come here for the last few visits," Raina remarked. "Princess Lolli must be excited." She looked over at Candy Castle. "I wonder if she gets nervous about traveling such a far distance. I would!"

Berry reached for her fruit nectar drink. "I

saw Butterscotch yesterday. She was looking forward to the flight. If I could ride Butterscotch there, I wouldn't be afraid."

Butterscotch was a royal unicorn. She was a beautiful caramel color with a deep-pink mane. She often took Princess Lolli on long voyages.

"Maybe," Raina said thoughtfully. "I'm not sure that's a trip I would want to make with Butterscotch, or any unicorn."

"I would take a unicorn ride any day!" Dash said, landing next to Berry.

"Dash!" Berry exclaimed. "Lickin' lollipops, you scared the sugar out of me."

Dash giggled. "Sorry," the small Mint Fairy said. "When Raina told me she was meeting you for lunch, I had to join in the fun."

"And so did we!" Melli said, flying in with Cocoa.

Berry looked at the Caramel and Chocolate Fairies in front of her. "You came to see me?"

"Sure as sugar!" Cocoa said. "We missed you last night."

"Were you talking about Princess Lolli's trip?" Melli asked. She sat down next to Berry. "I know Berry wishes she could go. Besides Meringue Island, Cake Kingdom is the leading place for fashion, right, Berry?"

Berry shrugged. "Well, Cake Kingdom does have some sweet styles," she said, thinking. "But I've never been there. I've only read about it in *Sugar Beat* magazine."

The five fairy friends settled down to eat their

lunch. It wasn't often that they got to see one another during the day. Usually, each of the fairies worked in a different part of the kingdom on her own candies. This was a sweet surprise lunch.

They had just finished eating when a burst of chilly air lifted Melli up off the ground. "Brrrr," she said, shivering. "What is going on? It was such a beautiful morning!"

"I think there's a storm coming," Cocoa said. She looked up to the sky and saw the dark clouds rushing overhead. "Bittersweet, I was so hoping for another warm night."

"That isn't going to happen," Dash said, slipping on her vest. She carefully wiggled her silver wings through the slots in the back. "Nothing like a brisk spring evening to get the mint flowing," she added. "And I have got some mighty mints to tend to. See you fairies later!" In a flash, Dash was gone. She wasn't known as the fastest fairy in Sugar Valley for nothing!

Melli wrapped her shawl tighter around her waist. "What about your seedlings, Berry?" she asked. "They are not going to like this blast of cold."

"Oh, it's not so bad," Berry told her. She looked up at the sky. "Winter has passed. Sure as sugar, the sun will warm us all tomorrow with another sunny day. I can't wait!"

Berry's friends shared a worried look. But they all agreed to meet up at Sun Dip the next day to put their candies and finishing touches in the basket. They knew Princess Lolli was counting on them. And none of them wanted to disappoint the sweet fairy princess.